Josiah and

The
Mystery
of the
Missing Football

Written by
Renee M. Carter

Illustrated by
Kalysaayln

Josiah and The Mystery of the Missing Football

No part or parts of this publication may be scanned, reproduced in part or in whole, nor can it be stored in a retrieval system. No part or parts of this publication can be transmitted in any form or by any means, mechanical, recording, photocopying, electronic or otherwise, unless written permission is granted by the publisher. For interest in and details regarding permission, email Mustard Seed Faith Publishing @ mustardseedfaith2021@outlook.com

ISBN 978-1-7367952-5-5

Written by Renee M. Carter   Illustrated by Kalysaayln

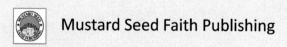 Mustard Seed Faith Publishing

Last night Josiah fell asleep thinking about his big football game with the Wildcats. Josiah's dad had to tuck him in because Josiah was too excited to fall asleep.

Game Ball

The Tigers and the Wildcats were the

best two teams in the

whole football

league. And today they were playing,

The Championship Game.

Tigers Team Captain

Josiah was his team's captain.
Josiah didn't want to be late for the
game as his team had trusted him to take
care of the game football.

Game Day

Tigers VS Wildcats

Josiah loved football.

He was so excited to be playing in

The Championship Game.

The next morning Josiah jumped up, got dressed in a hurry and ran downstairs to the garage to get the game football. Josiah kept all of his sports balls in the garage.

Once inside the garage Josiah rushed over to the sports box to get the game ball. But Josiah was surprised to find that the game ball wasn't there.

Josiah immediately started to panic.
Where is the game football?
Josiah started tossing all the
other balls out
of the sports box onto the floor. Josiah
just couldn't believe that
the game football wasn't anywhere
to be found.

Josiah remembered that he and his dad were just outside yesterday tossing the game football around. Josiah decided to look again in the sports boxes because that football just had to be there.

Josiah looked again and again through those balls and the game football was just not there. It was like the game football had just disappeared.

Maybe the football had fallen out of the sports box, Josiah thought. Where could that football be? Josiah was sad as he did not want to let his teammates down.

Then Josiah got angry, and he wanted
to cry. Josiah could feel those
hot tears starting to run down his face.
Josiah immediately wiped
those tears away.

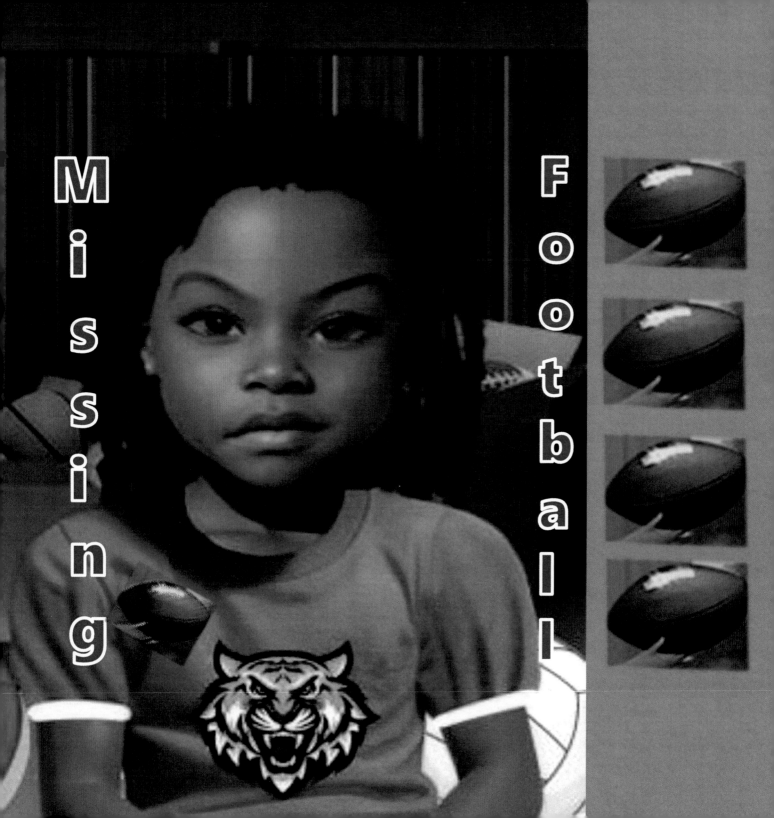

Missing Football

Crying might make him feel better, Josiah thought, but it would not help him find that missing football.

Josiah stopped and stood still for a moment as he remembered the last time, he had gotten angry. He remembered his dad explaining that everyone will feel anger sometimes, but you can't stay angry. He remembered his dad saying that you just have to know what to do when you get angry.

Count

o

u

n

t

BREATHE

Count

To

10

Dad said first, you must calm down.

Try breathing and counting to ten.

If that doesn't work, try counting to ten again and then maybe you will feel calm enough to think straight.

Tigers

Wildcats

Once you are calm,

figure out the problem and then you can

look for a solution.

Dad also said don't make important decisions when you are angry, because they most likely won't be the right decisions. Because those decisions will be influenced by your anger.

Game Day

THINK

Stop and Think!

What is the problem?

The game football is missing.

What is a solution? Remember there could

be more than one solution.

Find the game football, then

we can play The

Championship Game. 🏆

Wildcats

What would Dad do?

Josiah remembered dad saying it is

always ok to ask for help.

Dad says you

need to ask someone you can trust.

That's what I'll do, I'll go ask dad to
help me find the game football.

As Josiah ran towards the house, his dad was coming out of the house with the game football in his hand.

MISSING

FOOTBALL

Found

As Josiah's dad entered the garage,

he could see something had been

bothering Josiah.

What's wrong Josiah, his dad asked?

Josiah replied, "I thought

I had lost the game football."

Son, don't you remember how much fun
we had yesterday tossing that football
around?
Remember we decided to take the football
in the house for safekeeping.

Game Day

ON!

I do remember dad! I just got so angry when I thought I had lost the football. Then, I remembered what you told me, and I decided to come and ask you for help. Thanks Dad!

Great job Champ! Let's go beat those
wildcats. Josiah ran and jumped
in the car. He was ready for
The Championship Game. Josiah was
feeling happy again.

And the mystery of the missing football
was a mystery no more. For the
missing football had been found
and The Championship Game
has been won.

JOSIAH

FOOTBALL

Made in the USA
Monee, IL
04 November 2023

45437514R00036